The Wolf
Who Had a Wonderful
Dream

A French Folktale

Retold and Illustrated *by* Anne Rockwell

Thomas Y. Crowell Company

New York

Retold and illustrated *by* Anne Rockwell

The Dancing Stars: *An Iroquois Legend*
The Wolf Who Had a Wonderful Dream:
A French Folktale

Grateful acknowledgement is given to Alfred A. Knopf, Inc.,
for permission to adapt this story from *The Borzoi Book of French Folktales*,
selected and edited by Paul Delarue, © 1956 by Alfred A. Knopf, Inc.

for Lizzy

The wolf had a wonderful dream.

He woke up, yawned, and licked his chops.
He had dreamed of something good to eat.
But what?
He could not remember.

Out of his lair he loped into the sunshine.
«What *was* that good dinner I dreamed of?»
he asked himself.

Just then he came across a cheese lying in the road.
He sniffed the cheese and said,

4

«Surely not that!»
And he loped on down the road.

A shiny apple fell on his head.
«That apple was not in my wonderful dream.
It's probably sour!»
he said scornfully, and went on down the road.

He came to a loaf of bread.
He sniffed the bread and licked the crust.
He sniffed once more,
turned up his nose, and loped away.

Before long he came to a horse
eating grass in a meadow.

The wolf looked at the horse.
She was very big and strong,
but the wolf thought to himself,

«Could I have dreamed I ate a horse?
I've never eaten a horse, but they must be tasty.
And such a lot of horse!»
So he went up to the big horse.

She looked even bigger up close.
The wolf felt somewhat afraid.
But all the same, he bravely growled, and said,
«Horse, I'm going to eat you up.»

The horse looked down at the wolf and snorted,
«Well, if it must be, it must be.
But—I've got a thorn in my hoof.
Could you take it out, please?»

And because the wolf was not only hungry, but polite,
he agreed.
As soon as the wolf looked at the horse's hoof...

the horse kicked the wolf all the way
out of the meadow.

The wolf began to cry.
And as he howled sadly,
his empty stomach growled.

But soon he dried his tears   and went off.

He searched all day,

here and there,

for his wonderful dream.

Just when he was sure he would never find it he saw...

a big, fat mother pig
and four little piglets.
They were lying sleepily in a mud puddle.

«Piglets! Nice, fat, tender piglets!
That was what I dreamed of!
How tasty I dreamed they were!
Oh wonderful day!»

And the wolf drooled, and licked his chops,
and giggled with joy.
He loped up to the mud puddle.
«Mother Pig,» he growled,
«I'm going to eat up all your little piglets!
My, they *are* nice and fat!»

The mother pig began to cry.
But all the time that she was crying,
she was thinking hard.

At last she sniffled and said,
«Well, if it must be, it must be.
But just look at them! How dirty they are!
Surely you could not eat such dirty piglets!»

The wolf looked down at the piglets,
still snoozing in the mud puddle.
Truly they were very, very dirty.

«Of course,» said the mother pig, still sobbing softly,
«You could give them a bath.»
«Of course!» shouted the wolf happily,

and he fetched brown soap,
and a scrub brush,
and four soft towels.

All the while he thought to himself,
« Those little pigs will taste even better
when they are nice and clean.
My wonderful dream is coming true ! »
And he hummed a little song on his way
to the mud puddle.

The wolf, the mother pig, and the muddy little piglets
went down to the river.

And the wolf washed
and scrubbed those little piglets

until they were pink and shiny
and slippery with soap suds.

And when they were as pink and shiny and slippery
as they could be, the mother pig called,
«Swim, my piglets! Swim home to the barn!»

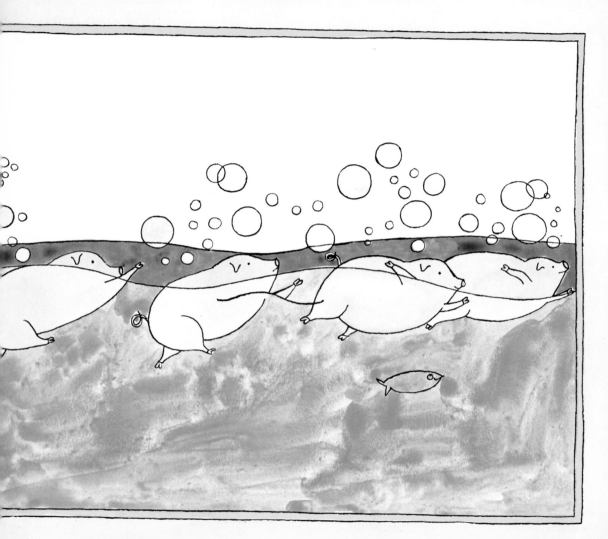

The little piglets swam away.
They were so slippery the wolf couldn't hold them.
Besides, he had never learned to swim.

So he loped on home to his lair, that wolf did,

and he had nothing to eat all day.

But that night he had another wonderful dream.

About the Author-Illustrator

Anne Rockwell spent a summer in Normandy, sketchbook in hand, drawing the farms, the *manoirs,* the people and the countryside, so that her full-color illustrations for this book would accurately reflect the special character of this unique and lovely part of France. *The Wolf Who Had a Wonderful Dream* is an old French folktale, which she has retold in easy words for the very youngest reader, while retaining the flavor of the original.

Mrs. Rockwell has known since she was a little girl that she wanted to be an artist and she has now written and/or illustrated many, many books for young people, including *Munachar & Manachar,* an Irish folktale as told by Joseph Jacobs; and *The Dancing Stars,* her own retelling of an Iroquois legend. She loves to travel and often combines her research for a book with a family vacation in some faraway spot. Anne Rockwell's husband is also an artist, and they have three children. The Rockwells live in Old Greenwich, Connecticut.